# THE THOMAS
# FAMILY VALUES

# THE THOMAS FAMILY VALUES

## Phil Anderson

authorHOUSE®

*AuthorHouse™*
*1663 Liberty Drive*
*Bloomington, IN 47403*
*www.authorhouse.com*
*Phone: 1-800-839-8640*

*Published by AuthorHouse    06/21/2012*

*ISBN: 978-1-4772-2529-5 (sc)*
*ISBN: 978-1-4772-1225-7 (e)*

*Library of Congress Control Number: 2012910936*

This book is dedicated to Ms. Shirley and her 2005-2006 fifth grade class at School #14, in Indianapolis, IN. They began the school year as a special education class but ended it as just a special class. Thanks for the inspiration.

# Contents

# Preface

The Thomas Family Values is a collection of short stories about a year in the lives of pre-teen siblings, Andre and Tameka (Meka) Thomas. Through the characters the author speaks to some of the many issues facing our children at home and in school.

In today society, social and school issues are intermingled. And because of teaching constraints the students aren't taught how to deal with the social issues.

For instance more then half of black men ages 18 to 25 are either in prison or have a police record. And it is a fact that the high crime and incarceration rates are directly tied to high drop out rates and a high rate of absent fathers who are incarcerated.

The author believes students should be taught from a young age about the criminal justice system and what the lifelong consequences could be if you enter into it.

The Thomas Family Values addresses that issue and others through a way children understand "the family". The author attempts to show through the children's thoughts, words and actions what it feels and sounds like not to have a father around or to encounter racism.

In the book the author emphasizes relationships between teachers and students and how intentionally or unintentionally a teacher can break a students confidence. All of these issues are important to children but they don't tell their parents because they are too immature to understand there is an issue or have a fear they may be punished or ridiculed.

In school there is no class about "feelings/emotions" or the importance of humanity and helping others. The Thomas Family Values attempts to convey emotions by including storylines in which others show compassion and concern for Meka and Andre. And they in turn learn that it's alright and rewarding to help others when they show compassion.

The stories are short and written in plain spoken language so readers of all ages and education levels can enjoy them.

The author does not claim the Thomas family stories are the answer to society's woes. However they do give informed insight into issues concerning our youth, while generating conversation with the questions at the end of each story.

# Introduction

The Thomas Family short stories give a view of family life not often portrayed in books, TV or movies. The family consists of the mom, Tonya Thomas and her kids, 11 year old son Andre (A.J.) and daughter Tameka (Meka) 9. The stories are about a year in the life of the kids, and how different events affect their school and home life.

# Chapter One

# Brand New

A new school year is all about new, new clothes, classmates and teachers. Tameka and Andre Thomas know the new school year is coming but they look at it differently.

Tameka, a confident, easy going 9 year old is starting the fourth grade and loves school. She has problems with her class work, but keeps it to herself. Meka as they call her is getting tall and believes she can one day be America's Next Top Model.

Eleven year old Andre James Thomas is starting the 6th grade and hates to see school start. He has few friends and is smart, which can be a problem in urban schools. In his last class the boys called him white boy and a sell out because he was smart.

Andre or A.J., as some call him, wonders if a lot of kids from last year will be back. Or, will he have a lot of new kids in his class. People move in and out of his neighborhood so fast, it's hard to keep friendships.

Their mom, Tonya a 28-year-old single parent is also ready for school to start. Tonya, a hairdresser, shuffles her appointments so the kids don't spend a lot of time alone. She doesn't want them to make the same mistakes she made so she stays on top of them.

As a senior in high school Tonya was pregnant with Andre and then again with Meka the year after she graduated. She got good grades and could have gone to college but that idea died with the birth of the kids.

Tonya hasn't seen the kids' father in years. He has been incarcerated for selling drugs. This is the Thomas family and they are like a lot of families in America today.

# <u>**Discussion Questions**</u>

Does the Thomas Family sound like a family you know?

Do you like school? If yes why, if no why not.

# Chapter Two

# Lost

While walking home from the bus stop, Tameka noticed a little boy alone and crying. She started to keep walking, but something inside her told her to stop.

When she asked the boy what was wrong, he began to cry even more. Between sobs she could make out that he was lost. He had gotten on the school bus in the morning and thought this was were he was to be dropped off. Tameka looked around and did not see a school bus or an adult. She thought about it for a minute and decided to walk the boy back to her school.

As they walked back to her school Tameka started talking to the boy. His name was Chris and he was 5 years old. As they approached the school Tameka saw her principal Mr. Moore. Principal Moore asked Tameka what she was doing back at school. She explained she saw Chris crying, asked him what was wrong and he said he was lost.

The principal looked down at Chris who was now holding Tameka's hand real tight and started asking him questions.

"What is your mother's name and do you know her phone number?" he asked. A puzzled Chris looked up at Principal Moore and shrugged his shoulders as if to say, "I don't know".

Principal Moore took them to the office. He called Tameka's mom to let her know what was going on and told her he would drive her home shortly. He gave Chris some candy to make him feel comfortable and then began asking him questions again, trying to get some information.

Chris began to relax and tell the principal what happened. He did not know his mom's name but he did know his teachers name, Mrs. Allison. After hearing Chris's story Principal Moore made a few phone calls.

A short while later, in walks a lady, Chris' mom, Mrs. Henderson.

She looked worried and like she had been crying. But when she saw Chris she was all smiles and hugged him like a mamma bear hugging a cub.

Principal Moore knew Chris' kindergarten teacher Mrs. Allison. He called her and found out everybody was looking for Chris. He had gotten off on the wrong bus stop and was lost from there. Mrs. Henderson was very thankful.

Principal Moore told Mrs. Henderson that Tameka had brought Chris to the school after she saw him crying. She thanked Tameka and Chris gave Tameka a big hug.

Principal Moore became serious when he told Mrs. Henderson that Chris did not know her name, address, or any phone number for her. She said she thought they would teach him that in kindergarten. Without sounding irritated he asked her to step out in the hall so that the kids could not hear them.

He told Ms. Henderson it was her responsibility to teach Chris her personal information and knowing it would help in situations like this. She nodded in agreement and was grateful for the advice.

By now, Ms. Thomas had shown up concerned that Tameka still had not arrived home. Principal Moore explained what happened and said if Tameka had not helped Chris, he may have gotten into a bad situation. Ms. Thomas smiled and remarked, "Tameka is growing up." She has been taught to look out for others whenever she can. Everyone went home, happy things worked out the way they did.

# Discussion Questions

What do you think it was inside of Meka that made her stop and help Chris?

What would you do, if you saw a small child in danger or lost?

Do you think you should help others in trouble or just mind your own business?

Could you tell someone how to get to your home?

What lessons did the children learn?

What lessons did the adults learn?

# Chapter Three

# **Bullied**

"Hey kid, hold up!" the big boy yelled to the smaller boy. The smaller boy, Andre Thomas (A.J.) turned around looking frustrated and a bit scared. He knew who was calling him. It was Malik "Bay Bay" Johnson, the big 6th grader, who probably should be in high school.

"You got any change?" Malik shouted as he approached Andre. No, A.J. quietly but defiantly replied. "Well you'd better have me some money tomorrow or else!" Malik said. He was so close Andre could smell his hot dragon breath.

While on the way home Andre thought, "Screw him, I don't have any money and don't have a way of getting any". He thought I'll talk to Jay, he'll know what to do. Jay was Andre's older cousin and lived two blocks from Andre in a rougher area. Andre knew Jay was pretty tough.

"What's up family?" Jay yelled as Andre approached. He was always glad to see Andre. "What you doin over here?" Jay asked. You know Aunt Tonya doesn't like you hangin out over here. "Got a problem, cuz," Andre said. Then he explained the situation to Jay, telling him that Malik was a lot bigger and stronger. He told Jay that Malik had beat up two of his boys last week, but he was not afraid of him, which of course he was.

Jay went over Andre's options in his mind, he knew Andre had never been in trouble and didn't know how to street fight. He thought Andre could snitch Bay Bay out, but nobody likes a rat. Andre could fight him, but he might lose and get put out of school on top of it. Jay thought he could fight for A.J. or they could jump him and beat him down together, but that would make Andre look soft for having his cousin take up for him. After thinking long and hard Jay knew there was only one answer.

Jay said "cuz you need to talk to Mr. Simpson." Andre thought "yeah Mr. Simpson". Mr. Simpson worked at the school but wasn't a teacher. He helped the kids with reading and talked to them about staying in school and stuff like that.

Jay was down with Mr. Simpson because he had spoken up for him when he got into trouble. Andre asked Jay, "How would I start talking about it?" Jay replied, "Don't worry, walk up to him and just say I gotta problem". Mr. Simpson will take it from there. He is kinda like your pops. He knows when something is wrong. Not having a dad, Andre could only imagine what Jay meant.

As Andre walked home he felt better after talking to Jay. He knew getting Mr. Simpson or another adult involved was the best move for him.

But he wondered if I didn't have an adult I trusted then what?" He remembered hearing on the news about kids getting bullied and then hurting or killing themselves because they felt they had no one to turn to.

Andre thought "If I didn't have an adult like Mr. Simpson to talk to then I would talk to my mom, Pastor Jones or maybe the principal."

I wouldn't take the bullying as something to be ashamed of and I wouldn't be scared to talk about it. The person who is bullying me has the problem not me. I just need somebody to help solve their problem.

The next day at school Andre avoided Bay Bay like Hanna Montana music. He looked for Mr. Simpson and finally found him in the cafeteria helping out with the lunch crowd. Andre walked up to him and said "Mr. Simpson my cousin Jay told me to tell you hey". Mr. Simpson said "tell Jay I said to keep his head up and I am gonna come visit him soon." Andre didn't know what to say next. Mr. Simpson said, "What is it Andre you gotta go to the bathroom?" Then Andre saw Bay Bay walk behind Mr. Simpson with his hand out, mouthing give me my money.

Mr. Simpson must have seen the look on Andre's face because he turned and said in a stern voice "Malik, come here man." Malik sauntered over to Mr. Simpson and said, "What's up Mr. S?" Mr. Simpson said, "Do you know Andre?" Malik carefully said, "Yeah I know him." Mr. Simpson said, "I want you to look out for him". Make sure nobody messes with him. If they do you come tell me. And I am gonna try to get Andre to help you with some of your work like we talked about. You got that Malik? "Uh, yeah Mr. S, I got it, Malik said softly" "All right then get to class before you're late, Mr. Simpson said."

Mr. Simpson then turned to Andre and said "Malik has some problems reading and sometimes he takes it out on other kids." "He really needs someone to help him." Can you help us out Andre? Andre was thinking doesn't he understand Malik "Bay Bay" Johnson is a killer! But before he knew it he was shaking his head up and down saying "yeah I can help."

Mr. Simpson arranged for Andre to stay a half hour after school and help Malik with his reading. While studying Malik initially tried to intimidate Andre, but Andre said screw it, whatever goes down goes down. When Malik realized Andre was not scared of him he raised up off of Andre and they became friends.

And after a while something really cool happened, Bay Bay was not bullying anybody anymore. Andre thought this all worked out pretty well, I didn't have to snitch or get beat up and I made a new friend.

# Discussion Questions

Can you think of other ways Andre could have dealt with Malik?

What does the story tell you about Jay and Malik?

What was different about the bullying situation once Mr. Simpson got involved?

Have you ever been bullied? If yes what did you do?

Are you a bully? If you are always picking on somebody, you are a bully.

What are some signs of being bullied?

A child does not want to go to school.

A child has physical signs, bruises, cuts, etc of abuse.

A child wants to avoid a certain person.

A child does not interact with others.

# Chapter Four

# I Don't Know the Answer

Andre's palms were sweating; they would always sweat when he was nervous. He was nervous because he was in his math class and had counted the number of people before it was his turn to answer a question, His question would be question 10, (9 x 12 =)?

He knew he should have studied the night before instead of playing Xbox and then watching the game. Andre's thoughts were interrupted when his teacher Ms. Wilcoxen asked "Andre question 10 please?" when he didn't answer, she repeated, "Andre question 10 please?" Everyone was looking at him now. This made him even more nervous.

Andre mumbled, "Don't know." "Speak up" said Ms. Wilcoxen. "Don't know, don't care," Andre declared. Andre felt like the teacher was trying to embarrass him. Other students were laughing and talking out now, "Quiet!" The teacher growled. "Andre, am I going to have a problem today because you didn't study last night?" Andre replied sarcastically, "How do you know what I did last night?"

It was so quiet you could hear the clock ticking. Ms. Wilcoxen cleared her throat and calmly said "Andre Thomas get your things and go out into the hall to cool down." Ms. Wilcoxen knew Andre wasn't a bad kid. But, she couldn't let him show her up. She had to keep control of her class. Andre got his stuff and headed out of class to the little table outside the door.

Andre was sitting at that table thinking about what his mom was gonna say and do to him. She did not like getting calls from school. He was startled when he heard, "hey boy what you doing out here?" It was Mr. Simpson. He had helped Andre out of a tight situation earlier in the school year. He trusted Mr. Simpson.

"Stupid teacher put me out of class for nothing," Andre stated. Mr. Simpson laughed and said "let me get this straight, she's a teacher, she's getting paid. While you're sitting out in the hall missing the lesson, yet, she's stupid?"

Mr. Simpson asked again. "Why did she put you out of class?" I didn't know the answer to a stupid math question. I hate math!" Andre muttered as he looked at the floor.

"You're a smart kid Andre. What was the question?" Mr. Simpson asked. "Nine times twelve," Andre whispered. "Andre do you know that math and science are the basis for a lot of good paying jobs? The people who help LeBron James, Lil Wayne and Will Smith invest their money have a background in math." "Do you like Nintendo or Xbox?" Mr. Simpson asked. "Yeah" replied Andre. "Well, the people who make those games have a math background."

"Yeah, but they like math. I hate math." Andre stated. "I understand", Mr. Simpson said. "But sometimes we have to do things we don't like. That's part of growing up and being a man."

Maybe, if you practice and study math, you will start to like it." "Do you like counting money?" Andre nodded his head yes. "Of course you do, then you have to know math." Mr. Simpson said.

"Now lets practice on your times tables. But first you have to apologize to Ms. Wilcoxen". Mr. Simpson knocked on the classroom door and asked Ms. Wilcoxen to step outside. He told her Andre had something to say.

Andre apologized to Ms. Wilcoxen. Mr. Simpson then told her he would work with Andre to improve his math skills. Ms. Wilcoxen seemed pleased, she said, "Andre, you can not disrupt my class and you can't smart mouth me, understood?" Andre shook his head in agreement. He wanted to say something more but held his tongue. He hoped she would not call his mom.

Mr. Simpson got the times table cards, and he and Andre practiced until the class ended. He told Andre to practice at home and he would check on him later in the week.

Before he left, Mr. Simpson said, "you know Andre they say Black kids especially Black boys aren't as smart as other kids. But that's not true. Other kids may work harder at school work than Black kids but they are not smarter." "You are intelligent and can be as smart as anybody in this school." "You can be whatever you want to be, there's nothing you can't do". You just have to work hard.

About that time the bell rang for dismissal and Mr. Simpson was gone.

Andre thought about what he had said and didn't know what to think. All he knew was nobody had ever told him the things Mr. Simpson had said. He felt good about himself. He thought I will try harder and see what happens.

# **Discussion Questions**

What makes you feel good about yourself in school?

What makes you feel good about yourself outside of school?

Do you feel you try your very best in school, if no then why not?

Have you ever had anyone talk to you the way Mr. Simpson did?

# Chapter Five

# You Ain't My Daddy, I Ain't Got No Daddy

Tameka had the TV up so loud she could not hear the caller on the phone. And by the time she turned the TV down the caller had hung up. As soon as she put the phone down it rang again, "hello she said", the message said it was a collect call from Anthony (Tony) Roberts, a prisoner at Pendleton Reformatory. The charge would be $5.75. "If you want to accept the charges for this call press one." Tameka wasn't sure what to do, so she pressed one.

The man's voice on the phone said "hello, who is this?" She said "Tameka. And who is this?" The voice said "hi Meka, this is your daddy, Tony." Tameka said, "I don't know who you are but you ain't my daddy cause I ain't got no daddy!"

The man on the line paused, and then said, "Is your mother home?" Tameka said, "No she is at work." The man said, "Is she still doing hair at Grace's shop?" "Yeah," Tameka replied, "how did you know that?" "I told you, I'm your daddy," the man said.

Then Tameka said, "If you are my daddy when was I born?" "August 19, 2002" the man said. And with that Tameka started to believe something she would never let her self imagine, "I have a daddy." She continued, "If you are my daddy where have you been all my life?" The man said, "Well baby girl, your daddy got caught up in some mess a few years back. I have been in prison the last 10 years."

"Well, why haven't you written or called before now?" Tameka questioned. The man said, "I had gotten 30 years in prison and your mom and I thought it would be better if I just let you guys go on with your lives." At this point Tameka's emotions caught up with her and she began to cry.

Comforting her, Tony said he had thought about her and her brother everyday and wondered what they looked like. He told Tameka that he loved her and wanted to be part of their lives when he got out in the next year or so. He also wanted her and Andre to come visit.

Tameka said she would like that, then at that moment a recording came on and said, "Your call will be over in 15 seconds." Tony said he would call back another day, and then he was gone.

Tameka was stunned. She didn't know what to think or do. She didn't know whether to laugh, or cry. So, she did both. She couldn't wait to tell her mom and brother what happened. When she called her mother she was so excited she could not be understood. Finally, between sniffles she announced, "I talked to my daddy today!"

Tonya was floored, she had not told the kids anything about their dad. She felt he was doing too much time and didn't want to take her kids through that. Tameka told her Tony was getting out soon and wanted them to come and visit him. Tonya told her to calm down and said. "We will talk when I get home."

Tonya was speechless. Her friend and co-worker, Karissa Terry, saw the look on her face and said "What's up T, are the kids ok?" Karrisa and Tonya were like sisters, they went way back when Tony and Tonya were going strong. "Tony called Meka from the joint", Tonya nervously stated. "What? Girl no!" Karissa said. "What are you gonna do?" "I don't know," a worried Tonya said. "If Tony finds out Meka may not be his daughter he will kill me." "Girl, you gonna be on Maury," laughed Karissa! "Shut up K.T." Tonya laughed.

Meanwhile, back at home Tameka had a million thoughts going through her mind. Like what does my daddy look like? How long before he gets out? Will he live with us? She could hardly contain herself when Andre got home. "Andre, Andre!! Guess who called?" Tameka excitedly shouted! "What's up with you?" Andre said apprehensively.

"Daddy called Andre!! Our daddy called." What? Andre said, "quit talking crazy girl, you know we ain't got no daddy!" Gathering herself Tameka said, "Andre, our daddy called us." "He has been in prison and is getting out soon." Andre tried to understand what she was saying, "you mean our real daddy is in prison?" "Yes!!!!!!!!," Tameka shouted "and he's coming home soon, hugging Andre, I am so happy!" she cried.

Andre's eyes lit up bright as a full moon as he thought about the possibility of having a father. Andre was envious of other boys with their fathers. He had hoped his mom would get married so he too would have a father. But now, to have his real father coming home was something he could not comprehend. How do you imagine something like a father's presence and love if you have never experienced it?

# **Discussion Questions**

What do you think a father's love and presence means?

Do you think Tonya should have told the kids about their dad?

# Chapter Six

# Why Do They Do That: Part I

Meka Thomas was on cloud nine after talking to her father. Feelings came up in her that she had never felt before. But now it was time to refocus on school. Sometimes she could not focus on her schoolwork like she wanted; her mom was always on her to get it together.

Meka hadn't told her mom the letters in the words don't always line up correctly, so her reading and understanding of what she read was sometimes not quite right. She had to concentrate extra hard to stay on top of her work.

On this particular day Tameka's focus was really sharp, she was on top of her game and knew just about all the answers to the questions the teacher would ask. Before she would never raise her hand to answer a question but today was her day.

Her teacher, Mr. Harley asked a question Tameka knew the answer and her hand shot up quick as a flash as did the hand of Megan the smart white girl in class. Tameka's teacher did as he always did. He called on Megan or another one of the smart kids. To Tameka all the "smart" kids were white. Occasionally the teacher called on Martell the one smart black kid.

Tameka hadn't noticed or cared to notice before. But today was her day. She was determined to "start getting it together" as her mom would say. Mr. Harley asked another question and Tameka's hand went up again. But the teacher called on a "smartie" as she began to view them. Finally, Tameka got discouraged and did not raise her hand anymore that day.

After class she asked Mr. Harley why he hadn't called on her when she raised her hand. She told him she raised her hand because she knew the answer. Mr. Harley answered, "Tameka you are a nice girl. I did not want to embarrass you by calling on you. Tameka said ok. But she was not okay. She kept thinking what does he mean by that?

# Discussion Questions

Why do you think Mr. Harley did not call on Tameka?

Was he wrong or was he protecting her?

Do you think Tameka should tell somebody she is having problems reading?

If yes, who should she tell and what should she say?

Have you ever had a teacher make you fill the way Mr. Harley made Tameka feel?

What should Tameka do?

# Chapter Seven

# Why Do They Do That? Part II

The next day Tameka was still upset about what happened in class. She felt something was wrong but didn't quite know what it was. Tameka decided to talk to her friend Vetta. When she told her what happened, Vetta said "Yup, something like that happened to me too."

Vetta went on to tell Tameka, "When my mother and her boyfriend were having problems, I couldn't sleep, because of all the fussin and cussin." So I fell asleep in class. Ms. Clayburn caught me and we had words. She called me out all loud and stuff and then when I said something back, she put me out of class.

That Mr. Simpson dude saw me in the hall and told me he was starting a group of fourth and fifth graders who would read to the little kids in kindergarten. I had read with him in a group-reading thing we were doing in class. So he knew I could read real good. Mr. Simpson told me "if I would start doing better in class I could help him get this reading thing going." "Girl, I really wanted to do it too, cause my little brother Jucee is in Mrs. Johnson's class and I really like her.

I wanted to talk to her about my mama and her boyfriend one time. I like the way her hair is done. She dresses real nice. I want to be like her when I get big. Anyway, I started listening more in class and everything. I was really trying. But every time I saw Mr. Simpson he told me he would talk to Ms. Clayburn. I would see him talking to her too. She would always be shakin her head like she was saying no, I saw him talking to Mrs. Johnson too. "I wrote Mrs. Johnson a letter telling her that I am glad she is my brother's teacher and I want to read to the kindergarten kids with Mr. Simpson."

"Well, Brittany told me she heard Ms. Clayburn tell Mr. Simpson she did not want me to do the reading thing because I rolled my eyes at her." I don't know what she is talking about; I didn't even look at her. The reading thing didn't ever get goin! Now I am mad at Mr. Simpson and I can't stand Ms. Clayburn! When I asked Mr. Simpson about it he just said "your teacher doesn't want you to do it right now."

"So yeah I know what you mean girl," Vetta said. "I was trying to do what they wanted me to do. But they lied to me and now I don't wanna do nothing!" "Man that was wrong!" Meka said. "Why do you think they do that? Don't they want us to be smart; don't they want us to learn stuff?" Vetta said, "I don't know but it seems like they only like smart kids." Tameka declared.

# Discussion Questions

What should Mr. Simpson have done?

What should Vetta have done?

What should she do now?

Do you have a teacher you look up to?

Have you had any situations like Vetta's or Meka's?

# Chapter Eight

# Alicia

The situation in class had gotten really bad for Tameka since her teacher snubbed her. She didn't participate in the reading lessons and never again raised her hand. Her teacher Mr. Hartley became concerned and set up a conference with Tameka, her mom, Mr. Moore the principal and himself.

The issue of Mr. Harley ignoring Tameka did not came up. Nor did the fact she was having trouble putting sentences together properly. Tameka did not want anyone to know she had problems. She didn't want her daddy to think she was a loser.

When Principal Moore asked Tameka what she wanted to do, she replied she didn't care what happened. Her mom asked her if there was something wrong in class and Tameka said no. It was decided Tameka would be in another class with kids doing class work at her level. This was fine with her; at least she would be away from Mr. Harley.

After a few days in her new class Tameka noticed the kids in this class were a little different. There were older kids and some of the biggest troublemakers in the school. The kids seemed behind in all levels of their class work. "I will be a star in this class" Tameka thought.

The class always seemed to have kids talking out or moving around, someone was always in trouble. This class was very different from any she had been in.

When it was time to read out loud nearly all the students had trouble reading. Tameka had problems too but not like these kids.

There was one girl in class that really struggled when reading. Her name was Alicia. Whenever Alicia read it took a long time for her to finish one sentence let alone a paragraph. The other kids would groan when she read and called her Bubba Gump. And when the students were broken into small reading groups nobody wanted Alicia in their group.

Tameka knew what it felt like to be put down and snubbed from being in Mr. Harley's class, she sympathized with Alicia but what could she do? Tameka "thought why don't they help her instead of teasing her and putting her down"? Finally one day she had had enough and asked the teacher, Ms. Shirley if she could sit by and help Alicia.

With her teachers permission she moved into the empty seat next to Alicia and said "hi Alicia", my name is Tameka but my friends call me Meka, you can call me Meka". Alicia who was always looking down looked at Tameka, saw the sincerity in Meka's face and immediately had a big smile on her face.

Through the next month or so the two became fairly close in class but not outside of class. Even though communication was sometimes difficult between the two, Alicia and Tameka were good for each other. Tameka helped Alicia with her schoolwork and Alicia helped Tameka be more patient. Also Tameka's presence helped keep the other kids off Alicia a little bit. You could tell when she read aloud in class that Alicia was more confident in her reading. She even volunteered to read, something she had never done before. Tameka felt good for and proud of Alicia.

All that would change one day when Alicia's mom came to class to talk to Ms. Shirley. She told Ms. Shirley they would be moving and Alicia would have to change schools. Today would be Alicia's last day in class. Tameka was stunned at the news and asked Alicia what happened. Alicia told her their time at the shelter was up and they had to move to another shelter.

It took a minute before Tameka understood what she was being told; Alicia and her family were homeless. Tameka didn't know what to say, she hugged Alicia and told her she would miss her. Alicia gave Tameka a letter written in crayon that read

"Meka u r my bes freind my only friend, I will mis u". Luv Alicia

Tameka cried as she read the letter because she knew it took a lot of effort for Alicia to write it. Tameka told Alicia she was proud of her and loved her and then Alicia left with her mother. Tameka thought I will never throw this letter away and whenever I feel sorry for myself I will read it and think of Alicia.

# **Discussion Questions**

Do you think Tameka should have told her mom or the principle; Mr. Harley ignored her in class?

What should Tameka have said in the conference?

Why did Tameka say nothing was wrong when there really was a problem?

Would you help someone in your class who has problems?

Do you know what being homeless means?

Why do you think about the kids teasing Alicia?

## Chapter Nine

# N-Word (Nigger) Bill

D o you remember the first time you encountered racism or discrimination? Well Andre Thomas does. He will never forget it.

Andre's neighborhood was a racial melting pot. There were Blacks, Hispanics and whites. Although they all were different they shared one common thing, they all were poor.

With this racial mix Andre had a mix of friends as well. They played basketball together. Their parents knew each other but did not interact together. A lot of families had older brothers and sisters who went to school together, but they didn't interact either. Andre hadn't thought anything about it until this one day.

Andre was playing basketball with his friends who all happened to be white. Down the street comes old William Blue, the neighborhood wine head. He is harmless and many say he is kin in some way to Andre. He was called Blue because his skin color is very dark, almost blue black. Some of the older white kids were also hangin out. Suddenly, Andre began to hear, "nigger Bill come here!"

Now Andre was not immune to the N-word. He heard it all the time in rap music, as nigga, but he had never heard it like this. The older boys were laughing and saying mean and hateful things. Bill sauntered up to the boys and asked them for money. They replied "We ain't got no money for no old nigger!" Andre thought, well damn, I guess I'm a nigger in their minds as well.

Andre went over to Bill. He looked into Bill's fire red eyes and did not see any understanding of what was going on. He took Bill by the shirtsleeve and led him away. That was the last day Andre played basketball or any other game with the white kids. He understood now.

# **Discussion Questions**

Do you know what racism is?

Have you ever felt racism?

What was the situation?

How did you handle it?

If somebody called you the N word what would you do?

# Chapter Ten

# Let's Talk

It's Family Day at the Thomas house. Family day is an evening that the Thomas family, Tonya, Andre and Tameka spend time together. They haven't had family day in about 2 weeks. They sure needed one now.

Today's family day agenda was pizza and conversation. Of course Tameka started it off with, "Mom why didn't you tell us about our daddy?" Tonya said straightforwardly, "Meka I have tried to protect you guys from any harm or disappointment". I felt when the time was right I would tell you. Besides I thought your daddy was gonna be locked up for a long time." Andre said, "What did daddy do?"

Well, Tonya said, he couldn't find a job after high school. So he did something stupid. He sold drugs to support us. Unfortunately, he was caught and because of the way the law is set up he got 30 years. What do you mean by that Tameka asked?

Well Tonya said "The way the system is set up, because he sold what's called rock or crack cocaine he got thirty years in prison, if he had been selling what's called powder cocaine, he may have only gotten a few years."

The kids looked like they didn't really understand so Tonya explained because rock cocaine is sold and abused by Blacks. We get more time in jail then Whites who sell and abuse powder cocaine. It's not fair but that's the way it is.

Andre said yeah somebody in the bathroom said something about some rocks.

"It's trouble Andre, remember that and never let hear about you being involved in any way with drugs, it will mess your life up, got it?" Andre said, "Yeah, I got it."

Tonya went on to say she was pregnant with Meka when Tony got locked up. And she wanted a good life for them so she felt it was best if she stepped away from Tony.

She failed to say she had been involved with another man, Big Chris, Jay's daddy for a brief period of time. And she didn't know who Tameka's daddy really was. Also it was her parents who felt it was best she leave Tony alone. But that's another story.

Tonya did tell the kids how she and their dad met. How he was a high school sports star and had pro potential in football. She showed them his picture in their yearbook. Tonya reminisced about how close they were and how they struggled when he got hurt and everybody walked away from them.

She explained to them that Tony was really trying to do the right thing. But he couldn't get a job without a high school diploma. So he felt he had to do what he had to do to support his family.

Tonya and the kids talked until bedtime and agreed they would go see Tony in prison around Thanksgiving. After their conversations Tonya realized she had underestimated the effect not having a father had on the kids. She also wondered what they kids thought about her walking away from Tony after he was locked up.

# **Discussion Questions:**

Does your family have family day?

If yes what are some of the things you family does?

What do you think about Tonya walking away from Tony?

Do you think Tonya should tell the kids about Big Chris?

What do you think the kids are thinking about everything?

# Chapter Eleven

# College

Tonya Thomas was thinking about the conversation she had with the kids about their dad. She felt bad for not telling Meka and Andre about Tony but she wanted a better life for her kids. Tonya began to reflect on her life, the choices she made and the consequences that went with those choices.

She thought about her decision to have her baby and not go to college. She had wanted to be a nurse or a lawyer and was smart enough to have been either one. But she chose not to attend college and instead went to cosmetology school and started making decent money after a year.

Tonya didn't torture herself for her decisions, she had to do what she had to do. But here lately she began to play the what if game. She would think, would my life have been better if I had gone to college even with a baby in my arms? Would my kids be in a better school? Would we have lived in a better area? Could she have met and married a successful man that would have been a father figure and mentor to the kids?

Tonya thought there's nothing I can do about any of that now but what I can do is work my hardest to ensure my kids are happy and successful.

She decided she would inject college into the kids' lives. She would talk about college like it was the next natural step after high school. But how do you explain what college is to a 4th and 6th grader?

She thought college is a school you go to after you graduate from high school and there are many types of colleges. People go to college to prepare for work and in college you can study for a specific type of job. Doctors, lawyers, nurses, teachers and people who run big companies all went to college. Tonya thought that's a good start and I will build on that as they get older. She would get them into programs that prepare kids for college. Tonya felt better about her situation when she realized it was not all about her but also what it was gonna take for her kids to be happy and successful.

## Discussion Questions

Do you know what college is?

Do you know what consequences mean?

# Chapter Twelve

# Me You and Mrs. Bloom: Part I

As Andre and Tameka were walking home from the bus stop, a fire-truck rumbled by. "Man that was loud," said Andre. "Yeah and it's close to our house too," said Tameka. They looked at each other and as quick as the wind they were off and running towards home.

They made it home in about three minutes. Luckily, there was no fire at their home. It was a false alarm across the street at their neighbors, Mrs. Bloom's house. Mrs. Bloom was an older lady who has lived by herself after since husband died. She had children but they were grown and lived out of town.

Andre and Meka often went to Mrs. Blooms' to help her with house work. They did work like cutting the grass, vacuuming, and going to the store. When the kids were small their mom sometimes let Mrs. Bloom watch the kids while she ran errands.

The kids were glad it was a false alarm and not a fire at Mrs. Bloom's house. Since she was older and may not have gotten out if there was a fire. While standing in front of her house, Andre asked Tameka if she had seen Mrs. Bloom lately. Tameka said, "No, not for about a week."

Thinking something may be wrong; they went up to her house and knocked on the door. No one came to the door, so they knocked again. After a few minutes Mrs. Bloom came to the door. "Are you ok Mrs. Bloom," asked Tameka? Mrs. Bloom replied, "Yes, I guess I get kind of lonely around the holidays and try to keep to myself." "Are you sure you're ok Andre asked? "Yes, I'm ok." Mrs. Bloom said in a soft voice. "Now you kids had better get home, its getting dark."

As they left they both felt a twinge of sadness. They both yelled at the same time Mom!!!!!!!!!!!!! Ms. Thomas flew out of the house and asked the kids what was wrong? They explained they were feeling bad because Mrs. Bloom was alone for Thanksgiving and wanted her to spend it with them.

Ms. Thomas was touched at the sensitivity of the kids. She told them "Mrs. Bloom's children, Kevin and Lesley may come to visit. But if they don't she can spend Thanksgiving with us if she wants to."

She also told the kids how proud she was of them that they wanted to help Mrs. Bloom. The next week went slow for Andre and Tameka. They were anxious to help Mrs. Bloom but had to wait to see if her children would come in town. Tameka asked, "Mom, why don't we just ask Mrs. Bloom?" Mom said, "We'll give it a little time, we still have a few days to go." "The subject of Mrs. Bloom's children may be a touchy subject for her and we don't want to make her feel worse than she has already been feeling," Mom said.

It was the day before Thanksgiving and the kids were real antsy because they still had no word on Mrs. Bloom. They started to walk in to talk to mom and before they could say anything, she said "let's go see Mrs. Bloom" their smiles lit up the room when she said that.

They went across the street and knocked on Mrs. Bloom's door. It took a while, but she finally answered. Mrs. Bloom looked surprised when she saw the Thomas' standing there. She said, "Well come on in and have a seat."

They went in and Tonya said "Mrs. Bloom the kids wanted to know if you would join us for Thanksgiving dinner?" They want to introduce you to our family and want you around for the holiday. Managing a weak smile, Mrs. Bloom's she said she would be happy and proud to spend thanksgiving with them.

She went on to tell Ms. Thomas how the kids help her with her chores and how she looks forward to having them around. Ms. Thomas smiled and proudly said, "They're good kids, most of the time!" They decided the kids would come get Mrs. Bloom an hour or so before dinner. As Tonya and the kids left they felt a warm glow inside because they had reached out to Mrs. Bloom.

## <u>Discussion Questions</u>:

What do you think of the Thomas' asking Mrs. Bloom over for Thanksgiving?

Do you think you should help others?

Do you know what compassion is?

Can you think of a person in you neighborhood who may need help?

What do you think about Mrs. Bloom's kids not coming for Thanksgiving?

## Chapter Thirteen

# What Cha Doin in There?

Bet you never wondered what goes on in the boys' bathroom in grade school. Let's take a peak.

First, it's funky! Then it can be like a street corner with all kinds of bartering and exchanges going on. Let's look in while Andre Thomas is trying to go to use the bathroom.

"What's up A.J., need something?" "Naw, I'm good" Andre replies. "C'mon man, check this smoke out" the voice replies as he approaches Andre. The voice was LaMarcus Johnson.

Suddenly a loud voice booms, "Johnson, Thomas, what you boys doin in there?" It was Mr. Jordan, the 5th grade teacher.

"Using the bathroom," A.J. yells. "Well you'd better not be doing no business in there!" the teacher yells. Damn, Andre thinks to himself can't even go to the john without being hassled!

When A.J. and La Marcus leave the bathroom, Mr. Jordan stops them to talk. A.J. stops but LaMarcus keeps walking slowly at first then faster and finally he runs outta sight.

Mr. Jordan turns and looks at A.J. and asks, "Well?" "Well what?" A.J. replies, "I was using the bathroom. I don't know what he was doing." Andre walks away thinking to himself, the fifth grade wasn't like this, why is everyone trippin and coming down on me?

# **Discussion Questions**

Have you had any experiences like this in school?

Do people at your school sell drugs?

What do you think of Mr. Jordan accusing Andre of something?

What would you say if somebody tried to sell you drugs?

## Chapter Fourteen

# A.J. Roberts

Prison can be a dark and dangerous place or a place for recovery and redirection. The Thomas family will soon find out which way the prison system has shaped Anthony "Tony" Roberts, because Tonya and the kids are coming to visit.

Tony Roberts was a smart, athletic, handsome and charming young man who had a bright future ahead. As a freshman in high school, he played varsity football and basketball. How did he go from such a promising future to prisoner number 6878875? The details unfold like a recurring nightmare in Black America.

In high school Tony and Tonya were as tight as the nuts on the Brooklyn Bridge. They were the dream couple until Tony tore up his knee playing football his senior year. After his injury the college recruiters' attention faded. Tony was disappointed and distraught; he suppressed his feelings with drugs and alcohol.

Tony then began selling drugs, he was a small time dealer at first but because he was popular and Tonya became pregnant, he took it to another level. Then the nightmare became a reality. Tony was busted selling drugs to an undercover cop. They tried to get Tony to snitch on his people. When he refused the authorities threw the book at him and disgraced him in the newspapers. Tony was only nineteen years old, but he knew if he said anything about anybody his family would be dead, that's the drug game. Tonya's parents thought under the circumstances it was best if a pregnant Tonya and Andre step away from Tony.

Tony's' situation is similar to circumstances facing a lot of young men in the inner city today. Things don't go their way and they turn to the streets for help because that's what they know. They don't have a man to show them how to solve problems and be a man.

Take the instance of Tony's father and Andre's grandfather, Albert Jacob (Jake) Roberts who grew up in the 1970's. The 70's were a difficult time for black men. There was the draft which forced 18 year old young men into the military and then to the horrible war in Vietnam. The inner city was stripped of a generation of young black men. These men were called to military duty for "their country" and because of the brutal physical and mental toll the war took on the soldiers, many were never the same.

To make matters worse they were ridiculed when they came home for being in the war and because of racial prejudice Black soldiers could not find a job. This was a reality for Jake. When he returned after serving 4 years in Vietnam he couldn't find a job. The mental stress of the war also took its toll and Jake turned to drugs for relief.

Heroin (boy) was the drug of choice at the time. Jake like a lot of guys in his situation became addicted to Heroin. He was in and out of jail a lot. His life was probably saved when he met Tony's mom. After Tony was born Jake slowed down and eventually found a job.

He grew into family life. But the drugs and the war had taken years off of Jake's life and he died when Tony was only ten years old. His mother tried but she could not make a man out of a boy. Tony grew into manhood on the streets. The decision to sell drugs to support his new family was second nature.

When trying to educate young black men it's hard for society to understand that things that happened long ago have an impact on a person's life today. Tony is an example; Because of what happened to his dad in the 70's. He did not have that fatherly guidance to show him how to avoid life's traps and pitfalls. Now a generation later, Tony made bad choices and he is not there to guide his son Andre through a critical period in his life.

If the majority of Black Americans are to share in the so called American dream, society and individual families have to the answer the question, how do you replace a father's love, wisdom and guidance in a child's life? Many families have answered that question successfully. Unfortunately the high incarceration rate of African American young men shows we have a long way to go.

This is the reality of many poor Black, White and Hispanic young men. They are caught in a vicious cycle of drugs, violence, prison and unwed parenthood. Many men think this is normal but these situations hinder their future and the future of their children. This reality is what faces Andre, Tameka and millions of other Urban American children today.

We will begin to see their future soon, because Tonya and the kids are coming to pay Tony a visit.

## **<u>Discussion Questions</u>**

Do you think something that happened long ago can affect you now?

Do you know who your grandparents are? Do you ever talk to them about where your family comes from?

Do you know who your great grandparents are?

Do you know what city or state your family is originally from?

# Chapter Fifteen

# Visit

The day had come for the Thomas family to go see Tony in prison. It was a bright sunny Saturday in early December. The prison was about eighty-five miles east of town. Tonya and Andre were quiet and nervous as they made their way to the prison but Meka was happy as could be. She was singin and talking all the way there.

Tonya was thinking "boy what am I gonna say to Tony? I know he still looks good, probably been lifting weights trying to make a Michael Vick like comeback." She chuckled as she thought of all the fun they used to have.

Andre was also thinking about what he was going to say to his father. "He thought I am not gonna cry, I am not gonna let my daddy see me cry. I want my daddy to know I have tried to be the man of the house and men don't cry."

Meka was thinking "I am gonna show my daddy off once he gets out". I wonder if he looks like me."

She knew that not many girls even know who their daddy is. She was going to hold on to him and never let go. This was the greatest day of her life.

Tonya broke the silence by saying "we are almost there" and reminded the kids to be on there best behavior and to not be afraid of their surroundings.

As the drove near the prison they saw signs that read "don't pick up hitchhikers" and "caution approaching a prison facility". They also began to see the tall fences with razor wire at the top surrounding the facility. It was intimidating and scary all at the same time.

When they pulled into the parking area Tonya told the kids to leave wallets, purses and anything else in the car. She told them they would be searched. Andre said why "we ain't done nothing". Just another hassle like at school he thought.

When they went into the main building an officer asked their names and got identification from Tonya. He searched Tonya and the kids and had them walk through a metal detector.

He then led them to a big metal door where another officer let them in and walked them to a cafeteria-style room with tables, chairs and vending machines. By now the kids were pretty shaken by the whole experience. Going into a prison for the first time can be an eye opening experience, especially for kids.

But now they were there and had passed through all the hassles to see Tony. They waited a good twenty minutes and saw many men; most who were African American pass through the area. Finally they saw a handsome young man walking towards them; Meka whispered to her mom "is that my daddy?" That's him Tonya replied and with that Meka ran to him and jumped into his arms and hugged him for what seemed like forever. She cried and kept saying I love you daddy, I love you. Tony was also crying and saying I love you too.

Finally Meka took him by the hand and led him to Andre and Tonya. Tonya was always putty in Tony's hands; she melted into his strong arms like he had never been away. Andre was just looking, taking it all in. He didn't know what to say he didn't know what to do. After Tonya and Tony got through huggin and kissin, Tony looked at Andre and said come here man. He hugged Andre and "said it's been almost ten years since I last saw you". Andre still didn't know what to say, but he was thinking I ain't gonna cry, I ain't gonna cry.

Tony said son "this is a place you don't ever want to be in, got that?" Andre shook his head yes. With that it was complete they were a family. Tonya and the kids stayed their full allotment of time. They talked about every thing. They talked about how Tonya and Tony met. They talked about what kind of stuff he did in prison and what he ate. The kids told their dad things even Tonya didn't know

They also took a family picture, which of course Meka held onto. Tonya was surprised and pleased at how Tony looked and sounded. He had matured into a man and was not the selfish, tortured former athlete he was when she last saw him. While in prison he had completed his high school education and had earned a certification in auto body repair.

Tony was getting out sometime within the next year. But he knew it wasn't the time to talk about what happens when he gets out. However he let Tonya know he wanted to be with her and the kids.

As the time approached for them to leave, Tameka got real quiet. She held on to her dad and cried I don't wanna leave. While looking at Tonya, Tony told her "don't be sad this is just the first visit, we will be seeing a lot of each other, and we are a family now". Tonya had the look that said yes we will be back and they began to leave. While walking back to the main room Andre turned around and looked at his dad, he suddenly ran back to him and hugged him. Then with tears streaming down his face cried "I love you daddy." Tony said "I love you to son, keep the family together until I get out". Tonya and the kids then walked back through the big steel door and were back in the main waiting room.

On the ride back home everyone was quiet and kind of sad, they hated leaving Tony there. Tonya once again broke the silence saying "well what do you guys think of your daddy?" Meka spoke up first," mama I can see how you got with my daddy he is the most handsome man I have ever seen" I wanna come visit him every weekend. Tonya laughed while saying we can't come every weekend, but we will be back.

She turned to Andre and said "what about your Andre, what do you make of you dad?" I don't know what to think, he said. I have never had a daddy before; I know I want him around. He's big and strong and looks like nobody messes with him. He then said "I hate that prison, it reminds me of school and they way they treat us'. Yeah me too said Meka. She said what about you mama, what did you think of our daddy? With a warm smile Tonya said I never stopped lovin your daddy, that's why I could never get serious about anyone else.

They drove back to home in silence each with their own thoughts about the visit.

# <u>Discussion Questions:</u>

What do you think about the Thomas family situation?

What do you think about the visit to see Tony?

What do you think will happen to Tony once he gets out?

## Chapter Sixteen

# Is God Talking to Me?

It was almost Christmas Day and Meka Thomas was still on cloud nine after visiting her dad in prison. She couldn't get over how everything had happened. She thought "I was just sitting at home chillin and the phone rings and it's my daddy". I had never heard of him before in my life. And then to actually meet him a few months later how weird was that.

While thinking and flipping through the TV channels she passed a religious station and the man on the television said "God is talking to you". Meka kept flipping through the channels but the words "God is talking to you" stayed in her head. She though with all this stuff going on with my daddy, could God be talking to me? Naw, she said to herself, I didn't hear a voice say anything to me.

For the next few days Meka kept thinking about what she heard on TV. She had been watching Christmas shows which dealt with the birth of Jesus and other religious subjects. Watching these shows raised questions in her mind.

Meka asked her friend Vetta do you think God talks to people? Vetta replied "I don't know but if He does can you please ask Him to talk to my mother and her boyfriend cause they are getting on my nerves". Meka then asked her teacher Ms. Shirley, Ms. Shirley replied sorry Meka, we aren't allowed to talk about religious matters in school. Maybe you should ask your mom.

Finally she asked her mom, does God talk to kids? Her mother said God talks to everybody, why did you ask me that? Meka explained how happy she has been since she met her father. She couldn't really explain what it meant but she told her about hearing "God is talking to you" on the TV and the questions she had since then. What questions do you have baby? Her mom asked. Meka went on to rattle off about ten questions that her mother could not answer. Her mom chuckled and said I don't know the answers to a lot of your questions but if you write them down I will try to get a meeting with Pastor Jones he will be able to answer your questions.

Pastor Jones! Meka thought. Even though her mom didn't take her and her brother to church every Sunday, Meka knew Pastor Jones and could see him in her mind in front of everybody in the church praying, preachin and sweatin. She never knew what he was talking about. But it made sense to the grown people. When her family went to church she would watch her mom pray and often cry. That night Meka wrote down her questions which included:

*Who is God? Is God a man, a woman, a person?*
*Is Jesus God?*
*Where did God come from?*
*Can we see God, what does God look like?*
*Is God the same for everybody, even in different countries?*
*Is God Black or White?*
*How does God talk to people? How do I know if he talked to me?*

*Why does God let bad things happen to people?*
*What does amen mean?*

The next day Meka was going to tell Vetta about her meeting with Pastor Thomas but Vetta didn't come to school. Meka thought Vetta is always at school, sensing something was wrong she went by Vetta's house. After finding no one there, Meka went home. Later Vetta called and by the tone of her voice Meka could tell she was upset. She said her mom and boyfriend had got into a big fight, the police came and bright lights were everywhere. She was ok but spent the night at her aunt's Ruthie's house and was too embarrassed to go to school.

Meka felt the pain in Vetta's voice and knew she needed someone to help her. Meka told Vetta she had to be strong for her little brother Jucee. Veeta cried but what about me, what about me Meka! Who's gonna be strong for me. They drink and smoke blunts all night long. I can't take it anymore. Meka paused and then said I am gonna meet with Pastor Jones soon and I want you to go with me. I know he can help us both.

# Discussion Questions:

Do you believe in God?

What questions do you have about God?

What else could Meka have done for Vetta?

What should Vetta do?

The school year is ending for Tameka and Andre Thomas. What was new is now old. The Thomas kids learned a lot in school this year.

But they also learned a lot about life. The lessons Tameka and Andre have learned will become part of who they are as adults.

Soon a new school year will be starting so look for new stories about Meka and Andre Thomas.